DRAGON MASTERS

CALL OF THE SOUND DRAGON

BY

TRACEY WEST

BRANCHES

SCHOLASTIC INC.

DRAGON MASTERS
Read All the Adventures

More books coming soon!

TABLE OF CONTENTS

THANK YOU TO ALLISON FALLIN AND JOE FALLIN

for helping me to craft Tessa's character, and who inspired me to make sure
this book could be experienced by readers who are blind or
visually impaired. I am also grateful to Joe Strechay for
his invaluable help in all aspects of this book. — TW

Text copyright © 2020 by Tracey West
Illustrations copyright © 2020 by Scholastic Inc.

Library of Congress Cataloging-in-Publication Data
Names: West, Tracey, 1965- author. | Loveridge, Matt, illustrator. | West, Tracey, 1965- Dragon Masters ; 16.
Title: Call of the sound dragon / Tracey West ; illustrated by Matt Loveridge.
Description: First edition. | New York : Branches/Scholastic Inc., 2020. | Series: Dragon masters; 16 | Audience: Ages 6-8. | Audience: Grades 2-3. Summary: The city of Remus is being torn apart by a duel between two wizards, and Drake, Petra, and Griffith have traveled there to assist a blind dragon master, Tessa, in sorting out the situation; using the sound dragon's unique power to manipulate sound waves, the dragon masters retrieve the Power Crystal which is embedded inside an unbreakable rock, but will it be able to absorb the cloud of uncontrolled magic that is threatening the city before it is too late?
Identifiers: LCCN 2019027525 (print) | LCCN 2019027526 (ebook) | ISBN 9781338540284 (paperback) | ISBN 9781338540291 (library binding) | ISBN 9781338540307 (ebook)
Subjects: LCSH: Dragons--Juvenile fiction. | Magic--Juvenile fiction. | Wizards--Juvenile fiction. | Dueling--Juvenile fiction. | Adventure stories. | CYAC: Dragons--Fiction. | Magic--Fiction. | Wizards--Fiction. Dueling--Fiction. | Adventure and adventurers--Fiction. | LCGFT: Action and adventure fiction. | Fantasy fiction.
Classification: LCC PZ7.W51937 Cal 2020 (print) | LCC PZ7.W51937 (ebook) DDC 813.54 [Fic]--dc23
LC record available at https://lccn.loc.gov/2019027525
LC ebook record available at https://lccn.loc.gov/2019027526

10 9 8 7 6 5 4 3 2 1

20 21 22 23 24

Printed in China 62

First edition, June 2020
Illustrated by Matt Loveridge
Edited by Katie Carella
Book design by Sarah Dvojack

THE WIZARD WATCH

right purple energy swirled around Neru
the Thunder Dragon. Eko, his Dragon Master,
stood next to him. The green Dragon Stone
she wore glowed.

Eko reached out with both arms. Neru's energy swirled around her. Then it poured out of her hands. Drake, Rori, Bo, and Ana watched with wide eyes, excited to see Eko use her powers as a Dragon Mage.

The energy from Eko's hands turned into a wall of purple energy.

"Cool force field!" Drake exclaimed. He had once seen Eko use Neru's energy to make a whip of purple light. But he had never seen her make a force field before.

"My connection with Neru is so strong that I can tap into his energy and use it," Eko said. "That is what it means to be a Dragon Mage."

She lowered her hands and the energy wall disappeared.

"That was awesome!" Rori exclaimed.

Bo raised his hand. "What exactly can Dragon Mages do with their dragon's energy?"

"They use that energy to perform some of their dragon's powers," she explained. "It takes many years to learn this. I can't create a Thunder Blast, like Neru does. But I can use his energy to make a regular power blast. Or create a force field, like I just did."

"Petra is going to be sorry she missed this," Drake said. "If I go get her, will you make another force field?"

Eko smiled. "Of course!"

It's strange seeing Eko smile, Drake thought as he ran to Griffith's wizard workshop. Eko had been Griffith's first student. She had made some bad choices in the past. But recently she had risked her life to save Drake and Rori from a dark wizard named Maldred.

Maldred had trapped
Eko in time with a bunch
of his wizard
enemies. The
Time Dragon
had freed
Eko and all the
wizards. Now Eko
was back in the castle,
helping Griffith teach the
Dragon Masters.

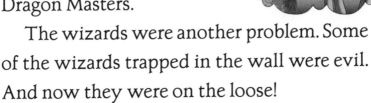

The wizards were another problem. Some
of the wizards trapped in the wall were evil.
And now they were on the loose!

"Petra, come see what Eko can do," Drake
told the curly-haired girl, who was busy
helping Griffith.

"In a minute. We're almost done with the
first part of the Wizard Watch," Petra said.
"Griffith looked in Maldred's journal and
found the names of the trapped wizards."

She pointed to a sheet of paper on the wall. "I wrote their names on this chart. Now Griffith is marking the bad ones."

WIZARD	HOME	EVIL?
Ezzie	Albion	
Calypso	Helas	
Baris	Turkland	
Astrid	Far North	✗
Berg	Misty Mountains	
Marco	Remus	✗
Gerik	Raging River	✗
Vela	Green Isle	
Katie	New Albion	

"If we find them, we can keep an eye on them in case they start causing trouble," Griffith said.

"That sounds like a good plan," Drake replied.

"Indeed," the wizard agreed. He turned to Petra. "I can finish this myself. You should go train with the others."

"Are you sure?" Petra asked. "I could —"

Boom! A loud sound erupted from Griffith's gazing ball. Rainbow light swirled inside the ball.

"What's happening?" Drake cried.

CHAPTER 2

TROUBLE IN REMUS

I asked the gazing ball to alert me of any unusual wizard activity," Griffith explained. He waved his hand over the glass ball. "It must have spotted something."

Eko, Rori, Ana, and Bo raced into the workshop.

"We heard a loud boom!" Bo cried.

"What's going on?" Ana asked.

Just then the rainbow light faded, and a scene appeared inside the glass. Everyone crowded around the gazing ball.

They saw a large stone arena with tall archways. It was shaped like a circle and open to the sky. The arena sat in the middle of a city.

"That's the city of Remus!" Petra remarked.

A strange red-and-yellow mist hung over the arena.

"That mist looks magical," Drake said.

Griffith nodded. "That mist is the sign of a wizard battle," he said. "When wizards fight each other, their magic builds up and gets out of control. That is why wizard battles are forbidden."

Petra checked the chart up on the wall. "Griffith, a wizard named Marco came from Remus!"

"Yes," Griffith said. "That is where he lived before Maldred trapped him."

"Do you think Marco is behind what is happening in the arena?" Rori asked.

"It is likely," the wizard replied.

"We need to stop that battle before somebody gets hurt!" Drake said.

"Yes, but remember: *Many* dark wizards escaped from Maldred's time trap. I will need some of you to stay here to watch the gazing ball," Griffith said.

"I'll stay behind," Eko offered.

"I'd like to go to Remus," Petra said. "It's close to my home in Helas. I know my way around."

"That will be helpful, Petra. You and Zera shall go," Griffith said. "As will Drake and Worm. We will leave right away."

"But . . ." Rori began.

Eko put her hand on Rori's shoulder. "We will keep watch, Griffith."

Drake, Petra, and Griffith headed to the Dragon Caves. Petra put a saddle on Zera, her four-headed Poison Dragon.

"We need to transport to Remus," Drake told his Earth Dragon, Worm.

His Dragon Stone glowed, and he heard Worm's voice in his head:

I am ready!

Drake, Griffith, and Petra touched Worm. Petra put her other hand on Zera's belly.

Whoosh! Green light exploded from Worm. They disappeared from the Dragon Caves.

Drake's stomach flip-flopped, like it always did when they transported. Usually he landed in the new place on both feet. But this time...

Whomp! He landed on something scaly! Drake tumbled backward. He opened his eyes — to see a big pink dragon!

TESSA AND SONO

Drake jumped to his feet. He had crash-landed on a dragon! Luckily, Griffith, Petra, Zera, and Worm had all landed just fine.

Drake stared at the new dragon. A wavy pattern of rainbow colors rippled across her scales. She had four legs and no wings.

A girl wearing a Dragon Stone rode in a
saddle on the dragon's back. She held on to a
strap that was attached to more straps on the
dragon's head and snout.

"Where did you come from?" she asked.

"Sorry I bumped into you," Drake said. "We are Dragon Masters, like you. My dragon, Worm, transported us here."

The girl's Dragon Stone glowed. "Is Worm the dragon with one head and tiny wings?"

"That's right," Drake said. "Are we in Remus?"

They had landed in front of a marble statue of a man with a helmet, sword, and shield. Behind the statue, a path led to the city that the gazing ball had shown them.

"Yes," the girl replied. "I'm sorry I can't stay and talk, but I'm in a hurry. My kingdom's royal wizard, Felix, sent me on an important mission."

"We came to stop the wizard battle. Is that your mission, too?" Drake said.

"It is," the girl said. "I'm Tessa, and this is Sono. She's a Sound Dragon."

"Tessa, we can help you! Can you tell us how this battle started?" Griffith asked.

Tessa turned her head toward Griffith. "Who said that?" she asked. "Sono told me that there were two Dragon Masters and two dragons. She didn't say anything about a man."

"That is Griffith, our wizard," Drake said.

"Why can't you see him?" Petra asked Tessa.

"I'm blind," Tessa said. "Sono helps me out. But sometimes she doesn't give me *all* of the details."

"Wow!" Petra exclaimed. "You and Sono work very closely with each other."

"Your bond must be strong," Drake added.

"That's true," Tessa said. "I hope to be a Dragon Mage someday."

"About your mission," Griffith interrupted. "Is a wizard named Marco back in Remus?"

"Yes," Tessa answered. "Felix told me that Marco grew up here, and that he became a dark wizard. He got into a fight with another evil wizard and then disappeared."

"We know," Drake said. "Maldred."

"Marco wants to take over as the royal wizard of Remus, so he challenged Felix to a duel," Tessa said.

"And Felix agreed," Petra guessed.

"No," Tessa said. "Felix knows that wizard battles are forbidden. But Marco started shooting magic at him and he had to defend himself. Now the duel has been going on for days and it's getting out of control!"

"We must stop this duel right away!" Griffith said.

"Yes!" Tessa agreed. "Felix said I should find a wizard to help Sono and me, so I'm glad I found you all." She patted Sono's head, and her Dragon Stone glowed. "Sono, turn around. Let's go back to the arena!"

The Sound Dragon obeyed and raced into the city.

WIZARD VS. WIZARD

ono and Tessa moved quickly through Remus, followed by the others.

"The road is curving to the right," Tessa said. "We're getting closer to the arena."

Stone houses lined the streets. Among the houses stood more statues like the one just outside the city.

"Remus is one of the oldest cities in the world," Griffith explained as they moved through the city. He pointed to a statue of a woman holding a dove. "That statue is Helen, a brave peacemaker."

"And there's Theo, who invented the sundial," Petra said. She pointed to a statue of a man holding a round disc.

Now the arena was in sight. It towered over the city.

Boom! Boom! Loud sounds exploded from the arena. Bursts of red-and-yellow light shone through the open archways.

Tessa and Sono reached the entrance first.

"Is everyone still behind me?" Tessa called back.

"We're here," Drake replied.

"Wizard, I hope you know what to do," Tessa said. "Their magic is out of control!"

Griffith stepped forward. "If it becomes too dangerous, we will retreat," he said. "We can leave and seek help from the wizards at Belerion."

"Belerion?" Drake asked.

"The castle there is a kind of headquarters for wizards," Griffith explained. "Also, young wizards go there to train."

Drake wanted to ask more about Belerion, but he didn't have a chance. Griffith stepped into the arena, and the others followed.

A crowd of townspeople had gathered to watch the battle.

Two wizards stood in the center of the circle. One of them wore yellow robes. His wavy brown hair was standing on end. The other wizard was short and round, with a blond beard and hair, and red robes.

"Sono, tell me what's happening," Tessa said, and her Dragon Stone glowed.

"Which one is Marco?" Drake asked.

"Felix is tall and skinny," Tessa replied. "And Sono says Marco is wearing red robes."

Boom! Red magic shot from Marco's hand.

Felix dodged the blast. He waved his hand and a horse made of yellow energy appeared underneath him. The horse galloped toward Marco.

"End this now, Marco!" Felix demanded.

"Not until Remus is mine!" Marco replied.
He pointed at the energy horse. It turned red
and transformed into a giant porcupine with
prickly quills.

"Ouch!" Felix cried, and he jumped off. The
energy porcupine exploded, and a lightning
bolt flashed in the sky.

Griffith turned to the Dragon Masters. "Stay back!" he warned them. "Their magic is already escaping from the arena. The whole city is in danger! I have to stop this."

Drake held his breath as Griffith entered the circle.

"Marco, Felix, enough!" he called out.

The two wizards looked at him.

"Griffith! Thank goodness!" Felix said.

Marco frowned. "This is not your business, wizard!" he said.

"I am afraid it is," Griffith said. "This duel must end."

"No!" Marco yelled. He hit Griffith with a sizzling burst of red energy.

Drake gasped.

A white duck stood in Griffith's place!

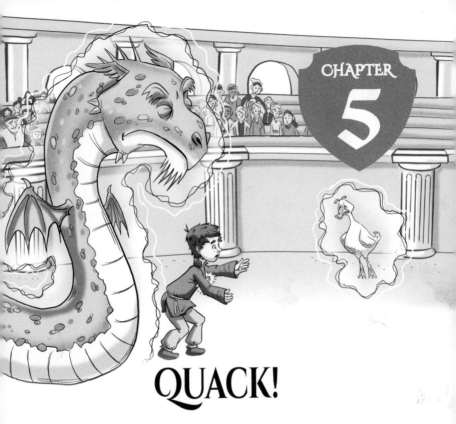

QUACK!

orm, get Griffith out of there!" Drake yelled.

Worm's body glowed, and the duck floated away from the wizards and into Drake's arms.

"Get to the city entrance as fast as you can," Tessa instructed.

Her Dragon Stone glimmered. The wavy pattern on her dragon began to wobble. Sono and Tessa shimmered and pulsed.

Then they disappeared!

Sono can transport! Drake thought. He put a hand on Worm and cradled the duck with the other. Petra kept one hand on Zera and touched Worm.

"Worm, transport us back to the entrance to the city!" Drake commanded.

In a flash, they appeared beside Tessa and Sono.

"Thanks for not bumping into us this time," Tessa said.

"*Quack!*" the duck quacked.

"So, it sounds like your wizard got turned into a duck," Tessa said.

"It looks that way," Petra said. "Unless he got switched with a duck, and the real Griffith is in a duck pond somewhere."

Drake held the duck in front of his face. "Quack three times if you are Griffith," he said.

"*Quack! Quack! Quack!*"

Drake smiled. "Good," he said. "I mean, not good that you're a duck. But at least we haven't lost you. We'll find a way to turn you back."

"How can we help him?" Petra said.

"We should go to Belerion," Tessa said. "That's what your wizard said. Felix told me to go there, too."

"*Quack!*" Griffith agreed.

"The Castle of the Wizards is there," Petra added. "I read a book about it once."

"Let's transport right away," Drake said. He turned to Tessa. "It looks like Sono can transport, too. But in a different way than Worm."

"Sono is a Sound Dragon, and one of her powers is that she can turn into sound waves," Tessa told him. "Sound waves move really, really fast. Do you and Petra want to try it?"

"No, thank you," Petra said. "I don't like things that move really fast."

"I'll try it," Drake said. "Worm, can you get Petra and Zera to Belerion?"

Yes, Worm replied.

"*Quack! Quack!*"

Petra laughed. "I think Griffith wants to go with me," she said as she took him from Drake.

Drake climbed up onto Sono's back.

"Put your arms around me and hold on," Tessa instructed. "Sono's going to turn us into sound waves, too. It will feel a bit weird."

Drake thought about changing his mind — but he decided not to. "Ready!" he said.

He looked down at Sono's wavy scales. They started to wiggle. Drake heard a humming sound in his ears. His body felt tingly. Then ...

... *whoosh!* They sped toward Belerion at the speed of sound!

6

BELERION

rake's head felt very fuzzy. They were moving impossibly fast. He felt frightened and excited at the same time.

This is really different from when Worm transports! he thought.

The tingly feeling stopped. Drake blinked.

They had landed on a flat, green plain, overlooking the blue sea. A path led to a tall castle that towered on the end of a cliff.

"What did you think, Drake?" Tessa asked.

Drake grinned. "That was a wild ride!"

"Right?" Tessa patted the braid of hair wrapped around her head. "That's why I wear my hair like this. Otherwise it flies all over."

Green light flashed, and Worm appeared with Zera and Petra, who held Griffith under one arm.

"*Quack!*"

"You beat us!" Petra said, surprised.

"Sono is really fast," Drake told her. Then he looked at the path leading to the castle. "That must be the Castle of the Wizards. Let's walk."

They stepped onto the path.

"So, Tessa, what other powers does Sono have?" Petra asked.

Tessa jumped off Sono's back, without letting go of the leather strap. "Sono has lots of great sound powers," she said, walking beside her dragon. "She can make powerful sound waves that can break up rocks. She can transform into sound waves and pass through solid things, like walls."

"She is a really cool dragon," Drake said.

"Is it hard being a Dragon Master if you can't see?" Petra blurted out. Her cheeks turned pink. "I'm sorry. Is that a rude question?"

"I don't mind you asking," Tessa replied. "The answer is that it's not hard. I have the same connection with Sono that you two have with your dragons. Just like you, I train my dragon. But unlike you, Sono tells me what's going on when I can't figure things out by what I hear or feel. She guides me and describes things to me."

"That's awesome," Drake said.

"Before I met Sono," Tessa explained, "I used this staff to help me get around." She pulled out the long staff strapped to her back.

"How does that work?" Drake asked.

Tessa let go of Sono's strap. She gripped the staff just below the dragon head carved on the top. Then she held the staff in front of her and walked forward. She moved it from left to right, tapping the ground.

"I move the staff a little wider than my body, to make sure it's clear for me to take a step. I can feel if there's a rock in front of me, or a door — stuff like that."

"That's so smart," Drake said.

"Thanks," Tessa replied. "I use my hearing and

other senses to get information about my surroundings, too. But having Sono as my guide is the best!"

"Sono's one of the coolest dragons I've ever seen," Petra said.

"Tell me about Zera," Tessa said. "What kind of powers does she have?"

"She is a dragon with poison powers called a hydra," Petra explained. "But she also has a beautiful song. She can heal anyone who is hurt by her poison."

"That is an amazing power!" Tessa said. "Can I hear her song?"

Petra smiled. "Sure," she said, and her Dragon Stone glowed. "Zera, please sing for us."

The hydra's four heads began to sing together in harmony. A sweet, pretty tune filled the air.

While Zera sang, Tessa's Dragon Stone glowed. A soft pink light shone from Sono. The light got brighter, and Zera's song became louder.

"That's another power," Tessa said. "Sono can change sound waves to make sounds louder or softer."

"Zera and Sono should experiment more when we have time," Petra suggested.

They had reached the castle. A wizard guard wearing a tall black hat stood in front of the door.

"Stop! No dragons may enter here!" he yelled.

THE CASTLE OF THE WIZARDS

The guard frowned and crossed his arms.

"You have to let us in!" Tessa demanded. "There's a wizard duel happening in Remus."

"And *our* wizard has been turned into a duck," Drake said.

Petra held out Griffith. "*Quack!*"

The guard raised an eyebrow. "Is that so? That duck sounds like an ordinary duck to me."

He bent down and looked the duck in the eyes.

"Quack! Quack! Quack quack quack quack!" Griffith scolded.

The guard straightened up. "Yes, Griffith! You can see the Head Wizard right away!"

"Can you understand birds?" Drake asked.

"Mostly just ducks and chickens," the guard replied. "You kids can go in. But your dragons must stay here. Those are castle rules."

"Sono needs to stay with me," Tessa explained. "She guides me."

"Quack quack!" Griffith added.

"Yes, guide animals are allowed," the guard said. "But Sono can't use her dragon powers inside the castle."

"Got it," Tessa said, and she and Sono moved past the guard.

"You'll find the Head Wizard at the end of the hallway!" the guard called after her.

Drake and Petra followed Tessa, leaving Zera and Worm outside the gates.

This place reminds me of Bracken Castle, Drake thought, looking at the floors and walls made of gray stone.

As Drake and Petra passed by half-opened doors, they saw scenes very different from those in Bracken. In one room, boys and girls waved wands with sparkling tips.

Right. Griffith said that young wizards train here, Drake remembered.

In another classroom, a boy pointed his finger at an apple and it turned into a potato.

Another room was filled with glittery purple fog.

Finally, they reached the door at the end of the hallway. Drake moved to knock on it, but the door swung open on its own.

They heard a voice from within: "Griffith! What trouble have you gotten into?"

THE HEAD WIZARD

rake and Petra stepped into the room, where a woman was sitting behind a desk.

The woman wasn't wearing a wizard's hat. Her white hair was pulled back from her wrinkled face. Instead of wizard's robes, she wore an orange dress with fabric draped over her shoulder. But when her dark brown eyes gazed at him, Drake shivered. He could almost feel the magic coming out of them.

"Hello, Drake and Petra," the Head Wizard said, and Drake was not surprised that she knew their names. "Tessa, please come in. But I'm afraid your dragon won't fit in the room."

"That's fine," Tessa said. She entered, using her staff to tap the floor in front of her.

"I am the Head Wizard. You may call me Jayana," she informed them. Jayana nodded to Petra. "Bring me Griffith."

Petra stepped forward and put the duck on the desk. Griffith waddled over to the wizard.

"*Quack! Quack quack quack!*"

"Oh dear," Jayana said, smiling. "I'm sorry to smile, my friend, but this is rather funny."

She clapped, and two wizards rushed into the room.

"Perform the Spell of Undoing on this duck," she told them. "He should end up as a human wizard when you're done."

One of the wizards scooped up Griffith. Then they both left without a word.

Drake frowned. "Will the spell work?"

"It will, but it may take an hour or so," Jayana replied.

"We don't have that much time!" Tessa blurted out. "There is a wizard duel in Remus, and it's getting out of control!"

"Is Felix involved?" Jayana asked. "He is not a rule breaker."

"Marco challenged him to a duel," Tessa answered. "Felix is just trying to save our city."

The wizard's eyes widened. "But Marco has been missing for years! When did he come back?"

"Maldred trapped him in time, but he escaped. It's a long story," Drake said. "Tessa is right. We need to act fast to save Remus!"

Jayana stood up and walked to a corner of the room, where a gazing ball sat on a round table. She waved her hand over it.

"Remus," she said.

An image of the arena appeared inside the glass. The red-and-yellow mist over the arena was now a big swirling cloud. People were running away from it.

The Head Wizard turned to the Dragon Masters. "You're right. This *is* serious," she said. "Only a Power Crystal can stop this magic."

"So let's get a Power Crystal!" Tessa cried.

Jayana shook her head. "I'm afraid that's impossible," she said. "And without a Power Crystal, Remus will fall!"

THE UNBREAKABLE ROCK

hy is it impossible to get a Power Crystal?" Drake asked the Head Wizard.

"I think I know," Petra piped up. "Any wizard who touches a Power Crystal will lose all of their magic forever! The crystal absorbs it."

53

"Correct, Petra," Jayana said. "The crystal contains the magic of all of the wizards it has absorbed."

"But we're not wizards, so *we* can safely use it. Right?" Drake asked.

"Yes, but the crystal is not easy to reach," the wizard replied.

She waved her hand, and an image of a towering rock appeared in the gazing ball.

"The Power Crystal is embedded inside this unbreakable rock," she explained. "And the spell to free the Power Crystal from the rock takes days to prepare. It will be too late to save Remus."

"Is the rock truly unbreakable?" Drake asked. "Worm's mind powers can break rocks."

"And so can Sono's sound powers," Tessa added.

The wizard shook her head. "Only the spell can break it."

"What if we don't *break* the rock?" Tessa asked. "Sono can turn into sound waves. We could pass right through the rock and I could grab the crystal and bring it back out."

"Of course! I should have thought of that," Jayana said. "Follow me."

Tessa climbed on Sono's back, and they all followed Jayana out of the castle, where Worm and Zera were waiting. Then everyone rushed down to the cliff's edge. An enormous rock as tall as a tree overlooked the waves.

Petra looked at the Head Wizard. "Are you sure going inside the unbreakable rock won't hurt Tessa and Sono?"

"They'll be fine," the wizard replied. "I think."

Petra frowned. "Tessa, maybe you —"

"I will risk it!" Tessa said. "It's the only way to save my city!"

Her Dragon Stone glowed. "Sono, we need to travel inside the big rock and grab the crystal inside!"

Drake's heart pounded as Sono's wavy scales began to move. The dragon and the girl began to shimmer. Then they walked toward the rock and seemed to melt right into it!

Drake held his breath, waiting for Tessa and Sono to reappear. But the seconds ticked away, with no sign of the Dragon Master or her dragon.

THE PLAN

Drake and Petra exchanged worried looks. *Tessa, where are you?* Drake wondered.

Suddenly, the rock began to glow with pink light. Tessa and Sono came out of the rock, wavy and shimmering. When they became solid again, Drake saw a glittering crystal the size of an apple in Tessa's hand.

"We did it!" Tessa announced. She held out the Power Crystal.

Jayana stepped away from Tessa. "I must not touch the crystal! Please hold on to it. It is very powerful, and you cannot let it fall into the wrong hands."

Tessa tucked the crystal into a bag hanging from her belt.

"Now," Jayana said, "let us return to the castle and see if Griffith is ready."

When they arrived at the front gates, Griffith walked out of the castle. Drake and Petra ran up to him.

"Griffith! It's so good to see you!" Drake cried.

The wizard hugged his Dragon Masters.

Jayana pointed to Tessa. "Griffith, this brave Dragon Master has freed the Power Crystal from the unbreakable rock."

"Well done, Tessa!" Griffith cried. He stroked his beard, and a few feathers flew out. "But Jayana and I cannot touch it."

"But *we* can!" Drake said. "We'll use the crystal to soak up all the magic from the wizard battle."

"And you wizards could get Marco and Felix to stop fighting," Tessa added.

"That's a good plan," Jayana agreed. "Drake, can you please ask your dragon to transport everyone?"

Drake nodded.

"Sono and I will meet you at the arena," Tessa said. Then she and Sono disappeared.

"I'll meet you there, too!" the Head Wizard said. And with a snap of her fingers . . . *poof!* She disappeared.

Worm transported everyone else to Remus. They landed outside the arena. Jayana, Tessa, and Sono had beaten them there. Frightened people ran screaming out of the arena. Overhead, the swirling red-and-yellow cloud looked much bigger.

"How do we use the Power Crystal?" Drake asked Griffith and Jayana.

"Uh-oh," Tessa said. "Do you hear that? Something big is coming."

She pointed behind them. They turned to see a giant statue as tall as the arena. It was alive, and it was stomping toward them!

A GIANT PROBLEM

That's the statue from the city entrance!"
Drake cried. "Only, it's enormous — and alive!"

"The magic from the battle has done this,"
Griffith said. "Jayana and I need to stop the
battle before the magic causes more problems.
Dragon Masters, use your dragons to stop the
statue! Then hurry into the arena with the
crystal!"

Griffith and Jayana ran into the arena.

Drake and Petra stared up at the giant stomping toward them. It carried a stone sword and shield. The ground rumbled as it walked. The stone street cracked under its huge, heavy feet.

How are we supposed to stop that*?* Drake wondered.

"Drake, didn't you say Worm could break up rocks, like Sono can?" Tessa asked.

"That's right!" Drake said. "But I'm not sure if his mind powers are strong enough to break a magical stone man!"

His Dragon Stone glowed.

I can try, Worm said.

"Maybe Sono can add her powers to Worm's," Tessa said. "First, we need to get the statue away from the townspeople before we attack it."

"Zera and I can handle that," Petra said. Her face was pale, but her voice was brave.

"Then let's stop this statue!" Tessa cried.

Petra jumped onto Zera's back. "Zera, fly!"

The hydra launched into the air. She flew up, up, up to the giant's face.

"Over here, giant!" Petra yelled. "Bet you can't catch us!"

The statue followed Petra and Zera, turning away from the city and stomping toward the fields. Drake and Tessa chased after it with their dragons.

"As soon as we reach the fields, I'll tell Worm to attack!" Drake called out.

"And when he does, Sono will join in!" Tessa called back.

The statue followed Zera and Petra all the way to the fields.

When they got there, Zera flew around the giant's head. The statue began to move in a circle, confused.

Petra and Zera flew away.

"Worm, now!" Drake yelled.

A green light swept from the top of Worm's body to the end of his tail. It grew brighter and brighter. Worm closed his eyes. Worm's green light snaked up the statue's legs, making cracks in the stone.

"Sono, break this giant into bits!" Tessa shouted.

Sono's body began to shimmer. Wavy pink lines poured from the Sound Dragon's body and wrapped around the giant.

The statue started to shake. Chunks of rock broke off and tumbled to the ground.

Tendrils of Worm's green light spread all the way up to the statue's head. Sono's pink light made the statue shake harder and harder.

"We'd better move back!" Tessa called out to Drake.

The dragons stopped their attack. Sono and Tessa raced away, and Drake and Worm hurried after them. Then — *Boom!*

The stone statue exploded into chunks of rock and dust.

INTO THE STORM

When the dust cleared, Drake ran over to his friends. They weren't hurt!

Petra's hands were shaking. "That was scary," she said.

"You did a great job drawing the statue out of the city," Tessa replied.

Drake looked back at the arena. The cloud of magic still swirled overhead, sparking and shooting out lightning bolts.

"Griffith and Jayana need us," he said. "Let's go!"

They raced into the arena. Griffith and Jayana were on the edge of the circle, floating in protective magical bubbles. They were trying to talk to the battling wizards.

Griffith zoomed over to the three Dragon Masters. "Marco and Felix will not listen to us," he said. "And we cannot use our magic to fight them. It will only make the magic cloud bigger. You *must* use the Power Crystal."

"How does it work?" Drake asked.

Griffith pointed to the sky. "You must take the crystal up there — beneath the magic cloud. The crystal will absorb the magic once you are close enough to it.  Just be careful not to touch the cloud. You may end up as a duck, or ..."

"Or worse," Drake finished.

Petra stepped forward. "Zera can fly up to the cloud, and I'll make sure she doesn't touch it," she said. "But one of you will have to hold up the Power Crystal to absorb the magical energy."

"I'll hold the crystal," Drake said.

Tessa held out the Power Crystal. "You two can do this!"

Drake took it from her. "Thanks."

He climbed onto Zera behind Petra.

"Are you ready?" Drake asked Petra.

"As ready as I'll ever be," she replied. "Zera, fly!"

Zera flew up over the dueling wizards. The very center of the magic cloud whirled like a tornado.

Flash! A lightning bolt streaked down from the cloud, and Petra steered Zera away from it. Then the dragon zoomed back toward the cloud's spinning center.

Drake held the Power Crystal above his head.

"Nothing's happening!" he yelled. "We need to get closer!"

Petra nodded and Zera flew up fast. One of Zera's heads almost touched the cloud!

"Slow down, Zera!" Petra cried.

Above them, a thin stream of the magic cloud twisted out toward the Power Crystal. It hit the crystal, which began to glow. The cloud swirled faster and faster, disappearing into the crystal.

Drake felt the crystal pulse in his hand. He added his other hand and held on tightly. Light beamed from the crystal as the cloud became smaller . . . and smaller . . . and smaller . . .

Until it disappeared! The crystal felt cool in Drake's hands.

"The magic cloud is gone!" Drake cheered.

A GOOD TEAM

Petra steered Zera back down onto the arena floor. Griffith and Jayana were still floating in their protective bubbles.

Bam! Marco shot a red magic blast at Felix. The wizard dodged it.

The bodies of both wizards sizzled with magical energy.

"If Felix and Marco don't stop fighting soon, they'll create another magic cloud," Drake said.

"They need to calm down," Tessa said.

Petra looked at Tessa. "Tessa, Zera's music might be able to help! Sono can make sounds loud, right? Can she control where they go, too?"

"Yes," Tessa replied. "I think I know what you want to do. Let's try it!"

At Petra's command, Zera began to sing a calm and soft song, like a lullaby. Sono controlled the sound waves of the song. She made the song louder and aimed the sound waves right at the two wizards. The waves reached the wizards.

Marco's hands were raised for another strike, but he slowly lowered them. His eyes drooped. Felix saw Marco's weakness and charged forward, but then he stopped. His eyes drooped, too. The two wizards swayed back and forth. Then they sank to the ground, fast asleep.

Pop! Pop! Griffith and Jayana popped the protective bubbles they had made. They landed beside the sleeping wizards.

Jayana pointed at Marco and silver light streamed from her fingertips. It formed a bubble around him.

"This will keep him trapped until I get him back to Belerion," Jayana said. "He will face judgment at the Castle of the Wizards."

"What about Felix?" Tessa asked. "He didn't *want* to battle Marco. He just did it to protect the city."

"He isn't in trouble," Jayana assured her.

"That's good," Tessa said.

"Now we need to get the Power Crystal safely back inside the unbreakable rock," Jayana said. "Tessa, would you mind bringing it back to Belerion?"

"No problem," Tessa said, and Drake handed the crystal to her.

"I'll meet you at the castle when you are done here," Jayana said. She snapped her fingers, and silver sparks showered over her and Marco. *Poof!* They disappeared.

Suddenly, Felix opened his eyes. "Marco, you'll never —" He sat up. "Marco?"

"He's been captured," Griffith told him. "And if you are okay, my friend, I will return to Bracken with Drake and Petra."

Petra spoke up. "Actually," she said, "I'd like to stay here in Remus."

A MESSAGE

etra, why don't you want to come back to Bracken?" Drake asked.

"Someday I will," Petra said. "But I miss my home, and Remus is closer to it. Also, I'd like to find out what Zera and Sono can do when they work together."

The two dragons were smiling at each other.

"I think that is a splendid idea, Petra," Griffith said.

Drake hugged his friend. "I'll miss you! We all will."

Petra smiled. "I'll miss you, too," she said.

She turned to Griffith. "You are the best teacher. Thank you."

"Felix is a good teacher, too," Griffith replied.

Felix smiled. "Thank you, Griffith," he said. "I'll enjoy having an extra pupil."

"Petra and I will meet up with you after we take this Power Crystal back to Belerion," Tessa told her wizard. She turned to Drake. "I'm glad you all bumped into me and Sono earlier."

"Me, too," Drake said, smiling.

"Okay," Tessa said. "We need to go."

Petra frowned. "I'm still a little scared to transport with Sono," she said. "But I think I'm ready to try it . . ."

"Come next to us and hold my hand," Tessa said. "We'll be there in a flash!"

Tessa, Petra, and their dragons transported to Belerion in a shimmering wave.

Then Worm quickly transported Drake and Griffith to the Training Room in Bracken Castle. Rori, Bo, and Ana rushed to greet them, followed by Eko.

"You're back! But where are Petra and Zera?" Rori asked.

"Petra wanted to stay and learn from Tessa," Drake said. "She's a really cool Dragon Master."

"What?" Rori cried.

Ana frowned. "I will miss her."

"So will I, but I'm glad she is happy," Bo said.

"Announcing Mina of the Far North and her dragon, Frost!" Simon the guard's voice rang through the Training Room.

Mina marched in. Her Ice Dragon, Frost, followed her.

"Mina! You're back!" Drake cried. "Are you here for a visit?"

"I have a message for Griffith from my wizard, Hulda," Mina replied. "She has found Astrid."

"Oh no!" Griffith said.

The Dragon Masters looked at him.

"Who is Astrid?" Drake asked.

"She is Hulda's sister, and she is the most dangerous wizard I know," he replied. "Even more dangerous than Maldred!"

TRACEY WEST has written dozens of books for children. She has never met a real dragon, but she has met some wizards, and they were all very nice.

Tracey is the stepmom to three grown-up kids. She shares her home with her husband, one cat, two dogs, and a bunch of chickens. They live in the misty mountains of New York state, where it is easy to imagine dragons roaming free in the green hills.

MATT LOVERIDGE loves illustrating children's books. When he's not painting or drawing, he likes hiking, biking, and drinking milk right from the carton. He lives in the mountains of Utah with his wife and kids, and their black dog named Blue.

DRAGON MASTERS
CALL OF THE SOUND DRAGON

Questions and Activities

Why are two powerful wizards named Marco and Felix battling each other? Reread page 19.

Tessa cannot see. She uses her other four senses — hearing, smell, taste, and touch — to help her get around in the world. Think about how *you* use your senses to stay safe. For example, you might hear a loud sound and move away from it. How do your senses help you?

As Drake walks through the Castle of the Wizards, he is reminded of Bracken Castle. How are the two castles similar? How are they different?

Tessa hopes to be a Dragon Mage someday. What does it mean to be a Dragon Mage? Reread pages 3-4. What kinds of powers would Tessa have if she became one?

Petra decides to stay in Remus with Tessa. What could happen when their dragons combine powers? Draw a picture that shows Zera and Sono joining forces.